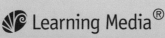

Learning Media®

PLATE POWER
BY DAVID HILL

ON TOP OF THE WORLD!

You've just scaled Mount Everest, and you're sitting on the summit, waving to airplanes and eating an energy bar. You've climbed the highest mountain in the world. No one on Earth will ever climb higher, right?

Wrong! A few million years from now, other mountains may be higher than Mount Everest. Mountains grow higher (and become lower) all the time. A mountain loses height when it's worn away by the wind and rain and when there's an avalanche. Even a climber can knock pieces off a peak. So, how can a mountain grow higher? The answer begins in the center of Earth.

ONION

Earth is made up of a series of layers – kind of like an onion. The middle layer is the core, which is solid and extremely hot – about 6,700 degrees Fahrenheit (3,704 degrees Celsius). The mantle, which is the second layer, is made from red-hot liquid rock. Most of Earth is made up of this molten rock.

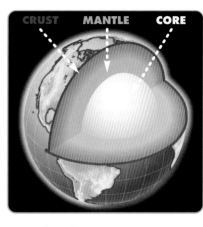

CRUST   MANTLE   CORE

The crust (Earth's surface) floats on top of the mantle. The crust is usually about 60 miles (100 kilometers) thick, but it isn't one solid piece – it's cracked into about twenty pieces, called tectonic plates.

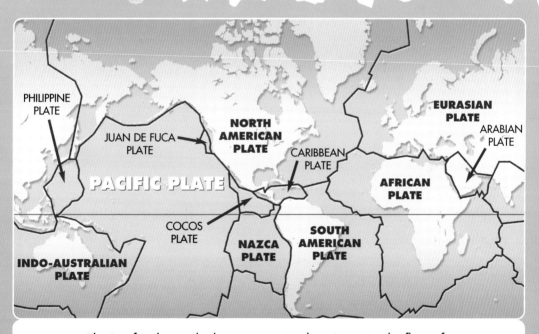

PHILIPPINE PLATE

JUAN DE FUCA PLATE

NORTH AMERICAN PLATE

CARIBBEAN PLATE

EURASIAN PLATE

ARABIAN PLATE

PACIFIC PLATE

AFRICAN PLATE

COCOS PLATE

NAZCA PLATE

SOUTH AMERICAN PLATE

INDO-AUSTRALIAN PLATE

The Pacific plate is the largest tectonic plate. It carries the floor of the entire Pacific Ocean. The North American plate includes the United States, Canada, and Greenland.

Earth's crust has cracked into these huge plates because the red-hot mantle underneath is always moving. Tectonic plates move incredibly slowly – up to four inches (10 centimeters) a year. This is the same speed as your fingernails grow.

Sometimes tectonic plates squeeze against one another, then move apart with a jolt. You might feel that jolt – it's an earthquake.

PANGAEA

Scientists think that Earth's tectonic plates may once have been joined in a huge continent called Pangaea. Around 250 million years ago, the plates began drifting apart.

If you look at the east coast of South America and the west coast of Africa, you'll see that they could fit together like jigsaw pieces. Fossils of the same animals and plants have been found in Africa and South America, suggesting that these continents were once joined. North America's east coast could also fit around the northwest bulge of Africa.

COLLISION

Some tectonic plates drift away from one another, some move toward one another, and other plates slide beneath one another. When these things happen, red-hot lava from the mantle may burst through the crust, and a volcano may form.

Usually, however, when two plates slowly collide, their edges begin crumpling upward to create mountains. Mountains are forced up by about an inch a year.

WHEN THESE PLATES COLLIDE, THE LAND BETWEEN THEM BUCKLES AND FOLDS.

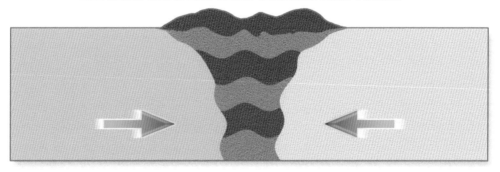

THE LAND RISES TO FORM MOUNTAINS.

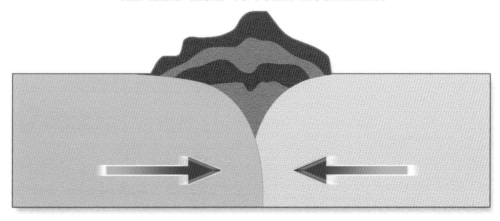

THE BIRTH OF MOUNT EVEREST

Seventy million years ago, while dinosaurs still roamed Earth, the Indo-Australian plate slowly collided with the Eurasian plate. Earthquakes shook the land, and volcanoes erupted. Land rose, and the Himalaya Mountains, including Mount Everest, began inching toward the sky.

Today, the Himalayas continue to rise because the Eurasian and Indo-Australian plates are still squeezing together. Mount Everest should remain Earth's highest mountain for a few more million years.

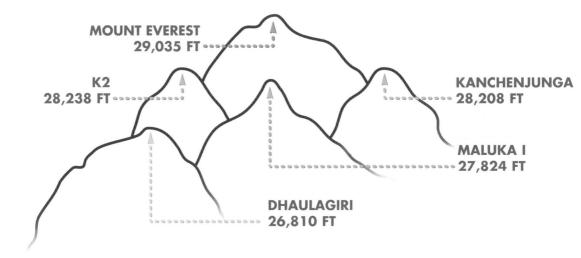

MOUNT EVEREST
29,035 FT

K2
28,238 FT

KANCHENJUNGA
28,208 FT

MALUKA I
27,824 FT

DHAULAGIRI
26,810 FT

- Mount Everest is 29,035 feet (8,050 meters) high, reaching 5.5 miles (9 kilometers) above sea level.
- The first person to reach the summit was New Zealander Edmund Hillary in 1953.
- The record for climbing Mount Everest is twenty hours, twenty-four minutes, set by a Nepalese climber in 1998.

IN THE FUTURE

In Africa, the tectonic plates have stopped pushing together. There aren't any new mountains forming, and the existing ones are being worn away. This is why Africa has so few high mountains.

Far into the future, Earth might look very different. California may have separated from the rest of the United States, and the Mediterranean Sea may disappear as North Africa nudges into Spain and Italy. A new ocean may form as South America and North America move apart. Meanwhile, Mount Everest may have stopped rising, and mountains such as the Andes in South America may have grown higher. Luckily, if these things did happen, they would take another seventy million years.

USA
Atlantic Ocean
Martinique
Cuba
MEXICO
Jamaica
Caribbean Sea
SOUTH AMERICA

The Caribbean

The Eruption of Mount Pelée

by Ali Everts

Mount Pelée, which is on the Caribbean island of Martinique, erupted on May 8, 1902, killing around thirty thousand people. One of the few people who escaped from the nearby town of St. Pierre was a young girl named Havivra Da Ifrile. This story is based on her experience.

I'll never forget those days in May 1902. Since January, steam had been rising from Mount Pelée's crater. Then in April, there was a series of small explosions and tremors. Ash pattered down on our homes and gardens, covering everything in a gritty blanket of gray.

Insects and snakes swarmed down the slopes of the volcano, and many farm animals died from the poisonous stings of red ants and enormous centipedes. My dog, Gerome, crept under Papa's chair and refused to come out for three days.

People began flooding into St. Pierre from nearby farms, where ash was ruining the crops and animals were starving. The city's leaders urged everyone to remain calm and stay in the town. Despite their reassurances, Mama was desperate to leave the island, but there was nowhere we could go.

Incredibly, everyday life went on. The townsfolk still went to work and visited their friends. On the morning of May 8, Mama asked me to deliver a package to Aunt Maria. "Hurry back, Havi," she said. "I want you to do some more errands later."

I waved good-bye as I set off down the street, unaware that I'd never see my mother again. I hadn't walked very far when I heard Gerome's paws padding behind me. I tried to shoo him away, but he was determined to come with me. "All right," I told him, "but you'd better not make me late." Gerome wagged his tail as though he understood.

I've often wondered what might have happened that day if Gerome hadn't followed me. My aunt lived near the volcano, and when we reached the lower slopes, Gerome gave an excited bark and dashed up the tourist trail that wound up the side of the volcano and into the crater. I ran after him, following his barks along the twisting path. I was angry because I was going to be late. I finally found Gerome scrabbling around the lip of the crater.

As I bent to scoop him up, I noticed dark smoke pouring from the crater. I crept forward for a closer look and couldn't believe what I saw. The crater below was alive, boiling red and flickering with flames. Squinting against the heat and smoke, I thought I saw someone crawling toward me, but it may have been a trick of the hazy light. The ground began trembling, and I realized how much danger I was in. Tucking Gerome under my arm, I turned and fled.

I ran as fast as I could back toward St. Pierre, the foul air
burning my throat and lungs. I'd just reached the edge of the
town when I heard a thundering roar. Glancing back, I saw a
boiling red wave surge over the edge of the crater and pour
down the slope toward the town. The lava spread outward,
churning and swelling until it swallowed the houses on both
sides of the road. Everything burned around me. The air was
filled with the wave's roar and the screams of people fleeing.

Thinking I might be safer in the water, I headed for the ocean. I shouted with relief when I saw my brother's dinghy bobbing near the shore. I waded to the boat, grateful for the cold water that soaked my clothes. I threw Gerome into the boat, then flung myself in after him. I grabbed the oars and began rowing out into the ocean, closing my eyes against the horror that lay before me. I desperately tried not to think about what might be happening to my family.

I don't know what made me think of the cave. Tucked into the cliff, it was the perfect place to shelter. During the summer, I'd spent many happy hours playing pirates there with my friends. Surely the fury of Mount Pelée couldn't reach me there.

I changed direction, hauling the oars toward the cave's
entrance. Suddenly there was a boom. I looked back at the
mountain. Above the town, the flank of Mount Pelée split open
like an overripe plum. An enormous boiling wave, much bigger
than the one I'd escaped from, poured over St. Pierre, engulfing
everything. Hot rocks and ash fell into the boat, burning my
skin through my wet clothes. Gerome shivered and whimpered,
crouching over the bow.

Choking with fear, I maneuvered the boat into the cave. Cool, dark air immediately surrounded me. It was quieter, too, although I could still hear the hiss of red-hot rocks plunging into the ocean. I collapsed on the floor of the boat, clutching Gerome and sobbing with horror and relief. The last thing I remembered was the water rising toward the roof of the cave.

Two days later, a French cruiser found my burned and broken boat drifting in the ocean. I remember nothing of those days. As they pulled me onto the deck of the ship, I was still holding Gerome, but his body was stiff in my arms. Looking back toward the smoldering ruins of St. Pierre, I knew that there couldn't be many survivors. I was one of the lucky ones.

illustrations by Dave Gunson

TSUNAMI

by
Maggie Lilleby

In 1992, an earthquake shook the Pacific coast of Nicaragua.
In the town of San Juan del Sur, people ran down to the beach,
where they watched in amazement as the water drained from
the harbor. Suddenly an enormous tsunami came racing in, and
hundreds of people and houses were swept away.

WHAT IS A TSUNAMI?

A tsunami is a giant wave that races across the ocean and crashes onto land, often causing massive damage.

Although tsunamis are sometimes called tidal waves, they aren't caused by the tides. They usually form as a result of an earthquake that has occurred near or on the ocean floor. Most earthquakes are caused by the movement of Earth's tectonic plates. An earthquake sends out shock waves that force part of the seabed upward. This creates enormous waves.

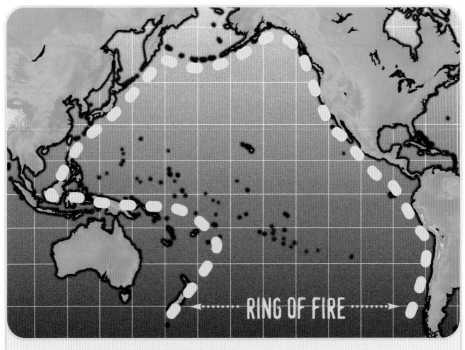

RING OF FIRE

Most tsunamis occur around the Ring of Fire, an area along the edge of the Pacific Ocean where there are many earthquakes and volcanoes.

FORMATION

When tsunami waves are traveling across the middle of the ocean, they're only a few feet high and there might be hundreds of miles between each wave. If you were on a ship, you might not even notice them.

A tsunami's speed depends on the depth of the ocean. The deeper the ocean, the faster the waves travel. Some travel at speeds of up to 500 miles (800 kilometers) per hour – almost as fast as a jumbo jet. That's just on the surface. Underneath, a huge volume of water is on the move. Tsunamis affect the whole ocean, from the seafloor to the surface, which explains why they have such tremendous power.

As tsunamis approach land and the ocean becomes more shallow, the waves begin to slow down. They are pushed upward, rising higher and higher. By the time they reach the shore, the waves may be more than 30 feet (10 meters) high. Tsunami waves don't usually curl over and break like regular waves – they are more like enormous walls of water.

Volcanic Eruption

Tsunamis can also be caused by the eruption of a volcano. After a volcano erupted on the Indonesian island of Krakatoa in 1883, several tsunamis swept halfway around the world. The waves rose more than 130 feet (40 meters), and many villages on nearby islands were destroyed. Thirty-six thousand people were killed.

1. An earthquake sends out shock waves that create huge waves.

2. As the tsunami nears the shore, the waves become taller and closer together.

3. The tsunami crashes onto land, washing away everything in its path.

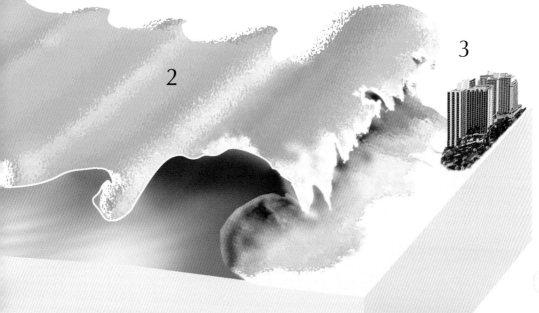

2

3

Effects

When a tsunami strikes, it can have devastating effects. The water can reach hundreds of feet inland, stripping beaches of sand, snapping trees, and smashing houses. Rivers and valleys leading to the ocean can also be flooded.

Tsunami Power

In 1960, a huge earthquake near Chile triggered a tsunami that killed around two thousand people and destroyed many homes. The tsunami swept across the Pacific Ocean, arriving in Hawaii fifteen hours later, where sixty-one people were killed. When the tsunami reached Japan, after traveling 10,000 miles (16,100 kilometers) in twenty-two hours, it killed a further 150 people. About 5,700 people were killed by both the earthquake and the tsunami.

WARNING CENTERS

Today, warning centers around the Pacific Ocean monitor earthquakes that may cause tsunamis. If a **seismometer** detects an undersea earthquake, a warning is sent out and people in the danger zone are evacuated.

Over the centuries, Japan has been struck by many tsunamis. In many harbors, concrete sea walls and huge gates have been built to provide protection from the giant waves.

SAFETY

If you're near the ocean and an earthquake or a tsunami warning is issued, you should:

- Move immediately to higher ground. A tsunami may only be a few minutes away.
- Stay away from rivers and waterways that lead to the ocean.
- Don't go to the ocean to investigate.
- Leave your home if it's in a danger zone.

 seismometer: an instrument that is used to measure the strength of an earthquake

Space Rocks!

BY DAVID HILL

It's nighttime, and suddenly you see a bright streak flash across the sky. Is it a UFO? No, it's a meteor.

Some meteors are debris left behind by comets. When a comet nears the sun, some of its dust and ice evaporate in the intense heat, leaving behind a trail. As Earth orbits the sun, it sometimes passes through a comet trail. If specks of ice or dust from the comet are swept into Earth's atmosphere, they become meteors.

 ## WHAT IS A COMET?

At the far edge of our solar system, thousands of icy bodies float in space. Sometimes these balls of ice, gases, and rocks are caught by the sun's gravity and dragged into its orbit, where they become comets.

Other meteors start out as asteroids, which are rocks that orbit the sun, mostly between Mars and Jupiter. Sometimes an asteroid is pulled toward the sun or Earth. When it enters Earth's atmosphere, it's called a meteor.

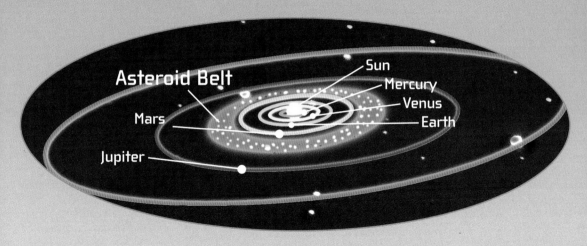

Most asteroids are found in the asteroid belt, which lies between Mars and Jupiter.

From Meteor to Meteorite

1. The fastest meteors rush into Earth's atmosphere at more than 60,000 miles (around 100,000 kilometers) per hour. As a meteor encounters the gases in the atmosphere, it begins to heat up.

2. About 50 miles (80 kilometers) above the ground, the meteor begins to glow white hot. This creates the bright streak we see in the night sky, which is why meteors are sometimes called "shooting stars."

3. Once they're in Earth's atmosphere, most meteors slow down and burn or break up before they hit the ground.

4. When a meteor falls into the ocean or onto land, it's called a meteorite. Some are large enough to make craters in the ground.

Craters

One of the most famous meteorite craters in the world is the Meteor Crater in Arizona. About thirty thousand years ago, a meteor 150 feet (45 meters) wide ripped through the atmosphere and smashed into the desert at 40,000 miles (65,000 kilometers) per hour.

The meteorite exploded, hurling white-hot pieces of rock for hundreds of miles. Dust and smoke turned the sky black. The impact created a crater 500 feet (152 meters) deep and 5,280 feet (1,610 meters) wide.

DEATH OF THE DINOSAURS?

Around sixty-five million years ago, scientists think a huge meteorite crashed into the ocean near Mexico, causing huge firestorms and tidal waves. Dust filled the sky for two years, and many plants and animals died. This impact may have killed off the dinosaurs.

In the past, thousands of meteors have collided with the moon, forming huge craters. These craters haven't changed in billions of years because the moon has no atmosphere and there's no wind or rain to wear the craters away. The biggest craters on the moon are over 500 miles (805 kilometers) wide.

Scientists have always been fascinated by meteorites. They search for them across deserts and the ice fields of Antarctica, where they have lain untouched for centuries. Meteorites are among the oldest objects in our solar system and can provide clues about how it was formed.

Slot Canyons

by Mandy Hager

Earthquakes, volcanic eruptions, and other mighty forces can cause sudden and dramatic changes to the land. Other changes, such as the formation of slot canyons, can happen over a long time, creating some of the most unique and beautiful landscapes on Earth.

Antelope Canyon

One such place is Antelope Canyon, a slot canyon in Arizona. It was created by the slow shift of wind, sand, and water over millions of years. Antelope Canyon is one of the most well-known slot canyons in Arizona, yet as you approach it, all you see is a small crack (or slot) in the ground. To enter the canyon, visitors descend a series of ladders and stairs.

Carved by nature into beautiful curves, the sandstone walls are magical. Orange, red, yellow, purple, and gray colors glow from the walls as light filters down from above. Flowing waves of rock curl and arch, and sometimes it's impossible to tell up from down or inside from out!

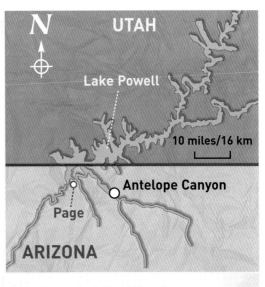

Antelope Canyon is near the town of Page, on the shores of Lake Powell. The canyon entrance is on the local Navajo reservation, and the Navajo are the guardians of the canyon.

In 1931, a twelve-year-old Navajo girl named Sue Tsosie was herding sheep when she discovered Antelope Canyon. The canyon is also known as the Corkscrew, Upper Antelope, the Wind Cave, and the Crack.

How a Slot Canyon Forms

1. Early in the Jurassic period (144–206 million years ago), the great Navajo Desert was created when northwest winds blew sand to form huge dunes. The sand eventually hardened into sandstone.

2. Over time, tiny cracks appeared in the sandstone. Water swirled in, and the sandstone eventually eroded to form round hollows. Softer material was washed away, and the surface became smooth.

Flash floods also helped to form the canyon because the hard ground couldn't absorb the large amounts of water. During flash floods, the water flows dangerously fast over great distances, collecting sand, rocks, and other debris along the way.

3. Eventually the rushing water and debris cut a channel through the wall of sandstone. These channels were shaped into a series of openings or slots, which are connected by narrow curved passages.

The deeper slots can be many stories high and impossible to reach. Some walls are only a few feet apart but drop a hundred feet or more to the canyon floor.

Sandstone Facts

- Sandstone is a type of rock made from sand that has been cemented together by pressure or minerals.
- The color of sandstone varies from cream or gray to red, brown, or green, depending on the minerals in the rock.
- Before concrete was first used, most buildings were made from sandstone. Sandstone isn't often used today because it's easily damaged by water.

The floor of a slot canyon is called a "dry wash." When it rains, the canyon turns back into a riverbed.

Safety

Flash floods are still a real danger in slot canyons. Five separate washes feed into Antelope Canyon, and so storms are taken seriously. If rain is forecast, the canyon is immediately closed to visitors. In August 1997, a flash flood swept through Antelope Canyon, killing eleven people.

The Guardians of Antelope Canyon

Slot canyons are rare and beautiful. They take million of years to form, and erosion is still shaping them today. Many people have visited Antelope Canyon, and because of this, parts of it have been damaged. Today, the Navajo people guide visitors safely through the canyon.

Find Out More

If you enjoyed this book, you can read more about **mighty forces** in these Orbit resources.

Chapter Books

Hawaiian Magic . . . . *NF*

Our Changing Earth . . . . *NF*

Remembering the Big Quake . . . . *NF*

The Scary Day . . . . *F*

Double Takes

Maui's Fish/
    Island Beginnings . . . . *F & NF*

The Voice of the Glacier/
    Volcano Watch . . . . *F & NF*

Shared Reading

The Birth of an Island . . . . *NF*

Our Changing Earth . . . . *NF*